To Luke : Ben :
You make the world
a better place and can
do anything you put
your mind to!

♡

Russell

The Adventures of Hope and Grace

Making friends at school

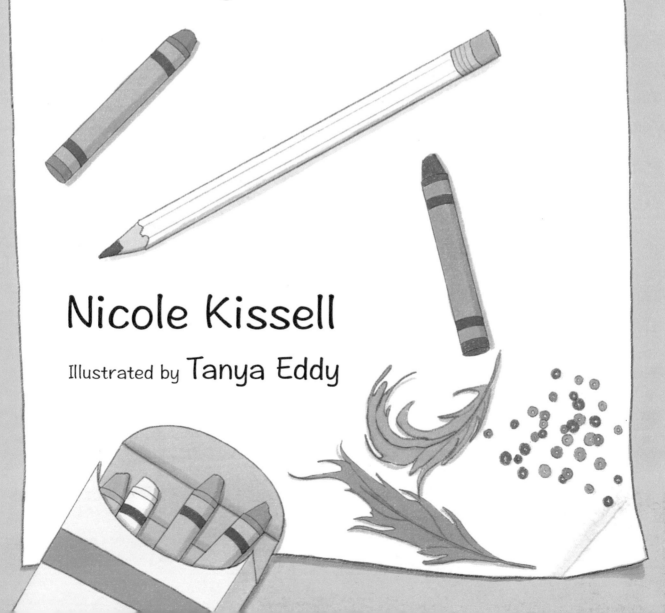

Nicole Kissell

Illustrated by Tanya Eddy

The Adventures of Hope and Grace: Making Friends at School

Hope and Grace Supply Co. books are available from your favorite bookseller or from www.AuthorNicoleKissell.com

Hardcover ISBN: 978-0-578-89176-7
Paperback ISBN: 978-1-7371859-0-1
Ebook ISBN: 978-1-7371859-1-8

Cataloging in Publication data on file with the publisher.

Illustrated by: Tanya Eddy
Layout Design: Rachel Thomaier
Edited by: Wildflower Books

Printed in the USA

10 9 8 7 6 5 4 3 2

It was the first day of school, and Grace was nervous but excited. She'd had a hard time sleeping last night, wondering what her classroom would look like, who her teacher would be, and what she should wear. Grace loved mix-matching fancy clothing, like tutu skirts with sparkly shirts, and her hair was always messy, no matter how much her mom tried to make it neat.

Grace entered her first-grade classroom. The desks were arranged
in groups of four, and a nametag and goodie bag waited on each one.
There was a cozy reading spot with a tent and pillows, and beautifully
decorated bulletin boards welcomed the children to their classroom.

Grace noticed one girl in her class who interested her: Hope. Hope had straight blonde hair and big blue eyes. She wore sparkly leggings and a sequined sweatshirt. Hope was quiet, but she seemed to have a strong sense of confidence. Hope was different from other children, and Grace was amazed by her.

Grace excitedly approached Hope. "Do you want to play?"
Hope froze and didn't reply.
"Why won't Hope play?" Grace asked their teacher, Mrs. Potter.
"Give her time," Mrs. Potter replied. "Some children play differently."

a mystery re

assembly

Love, M

Harrison

Hope

This was true. As Grace looked around the classroom, she noticed that some children played team games. Others liked to play in pairs. Some played noisy games. Some played dress-up games. But Hope played next to other children rather than with them.

"Everyone IS different," Grace said.

5

Grace saw that Hope had lots of fun keychains on her backpack and wondered how she had collected them all. "Wow! That's a cool LEGO keychain!" said Grace.

Hope smiled and told her she'd gotten it last year at the mall. Language was hard for Hope. What she'd meant to say was that she'd gotten it last night, but sometimes, she had trouble with her words.

7

Hope found her desk, which was right next to Grace's. The girls sat down and began to unpack their goodie bags. "Look!" exclaimed Hope. "I got pink Play-Doh! Pink is my favorite color."
Pink was Grace's favorite color too!

Next, Hope took out the crayons and began to line them up like the colors of the rainbow. This was one of the many smarts that Hope had: art! She was excellent at painting and drawing. Each person had their own smarts. Some had good LEGO smarts, math smarts, or people smarts.

day. We wil

reader

about kindness!

Mrs. Potter

Grace accidentally knocked over one of Hope's crayons, which caused them to tumble to the floor. Hope became upset and began to scream and cry. Sometimes, Hope had big emotional reactions to small problems.

11

Mrs. Potter approached the girls and helped them clean up the crayons. "Grace, let's take deep breaths with Hope to help her calm down," she said. "Breathe in through your nose to smell the flowers, and exhale through your mouth to blow out the candles."

Grace and Hope took three deep breaths together and noticed how calm they both felt. Next, it was time for an assembly in the gym! Assembly was exciting for most students, but Hope was scared to be around so many people she didn't know. Hope tiptoed to the gym.

14

When everyone was in the gym, it was very noisy! Hope started to rock, covering her ears.

Grace felt worried.

"It's okay," Mrs. Potter told her. "Lots of noise can be overwhelming for some children."

"What should we do?" Grace asked.

"I have these," Mrs. Potter replied, taking out a pair of headphones. "They're for Hope to use when it's too loud." Mrs. Potter handed the headphones to Hope.

Hope put them on and stopped rocking. Grace noticed a small smile on Hope's face.

After that, whenever it got too noisy and Hope felt overwhelmed, Grace reminded her to put her headphones on.

"Now, class, I'd like you to draw what you did on the weekend," Mrs.
Potter said one day.
Hope began twisting her fingers and chewing her lip.
"Let's line the crayons up before we draw," Grace suggested.
Hope smiled. She enjoyed lining up the crayons in color order.

Grace was amazed by Hope's patience and organization! Grace was often disorganized, always losing her materials. Her desk was a mess! But Hope's desk was perfectly neat, and she was always prepared. Grace and Hope were different in that way. That was why they made such a great pair!

As the weeks passed, Grace noticed Hope often sought her out. At playtime, Hope played near Grace. At reading time, she sat next to her. At lunchtime, she ate at the same table.

During art class, Hope created an incredible art project using different materials to create a rainbow unicorn.

Hope's classmates loved her idea so much that they all decided to try and make the same painting. They each included different materials, like colored paper, foil, and jewels.

"We're all different kinds of smart," Mrs. Potter said.
"Yes!" Grace called out. "Quincy is amazing at LEGO, I'm good at science, and Hope is brilliant at art!"

24

"What makes us different is the way our brains work. This is called neurodiversity," Mrs. Potter explained. "Everyone's brain is wired differently, so everyone has different strengths and talents." She asked the students to each create a book about their talent.

Hope was excited to write about painting. She asked Grace what she
was an expert at.

"Science experiments," Grace replied.

26

"Will you show me how to do a science experiment?" Hope asked.

"So long as you teach me how to paint!" Grace replied.

"Deal!"

"Hope smiles a lot more now," Grace told her daddy that evening.
"That's wonderful," he replied. "You do too, Grace."
Grace knew that her friendship with Hope was different. That meant it was even more special. She couldn't wait to share many more adventures with Hope.

Tips for Parents & Educators

Teaching children to celebrate diversity and include others,
is one of the greatest responsibilities we have as parents and educators.

---

8 Tips for cultivating kindness, empathy & compassion for oneself and others:

1. **Talk honestly and openly** about the many wonderful differences that make everyone unique. Discussing these differences can make the unfamiliar less scary and threatening, which can help reduce prejudice.

2. **Discussing challenging topics** can help children understand other people's life experiences better.

3. **Encourage children to work and play in diverse groups.** When students of diverse backgrounds are working toward a common goal and are treated as equals, and guided by the adults in their life to cooperate with positive and noncompetitive interactions, the children themselves are more likely to overcome their biases.

4. **Model being culturally sensitive.** As the adults in their lives, we can look at every interaction with our children as an opportunity to teach kindness and compassion. In our conversations with our children about emotions, differences, and actions, we can model courage, curiosity, openness, perspective taking, and compassion. Adults can set an example of tolerance and accepting other's differences. (Yale Center for Emotional Intelligence)

5. **Don't stare at or draw attention to unexpected behaviors.** In example, toe walking or hand flapping should be ignored since this is a way to express feelings.

6. **Be patient and allow the child wait time** to express their thoughts. Try to avoid jumping in to 'rescue them' and allow them time to respond.

7. **Practice mindfulness** to build compassion and empathy: have your child practice using positive affirmations (I am kind, I am loving, I am smart), practice mindful breathing to be in control of their emotions, and teach gratitude.

8. **Reward good behavior** when you "catch your child making good choices," and when he or she exhibits extraordinary tolerance or genuine concern for another, offer verbal praise, a hug or another positive gesture.

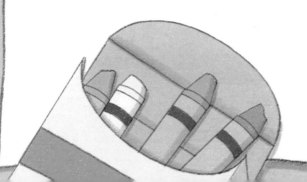

CPSIA information can be obtained
at www.ICGtesting.com
Printed in the USA
BVRC092215270621
610320BV00001B/1

* 9 7 8 0 5 7 8 8 9 1 7 6 7 *